When Summer Ends

by SUSI GREGG FOWLER
pictures by
MARISABINA RUSSO

PUFFIN BOOKS

For my daughters, Angela
and Micaela, and for Jim,
who nurtures us all.
With love—
—S. G. F.

For Thérèse and Patti,
Steph, and Aunt Joanne
—M.R.

PUFFIN BOOKS
Published by the Penguin Group
Penguin Books USA Inc., 375 Hudson Street, New York, New York 10014, U.S.A.
Penguin Books Ltd, 27 Wrights Lane, London W8 5TZ, England
Penguin Books Australia Ltd, Ringwood, Victoria, Australia
Penguin Books Canada Ltd, 10 Alcorn Avenue, Toronto, Ontario, Canada M4V 3B2
Penguin Books (N.Z.) Ltd, 182–190 Wairau Road, Auckland 10, New Zealand

Penguin Books Ltd, Registered Offices: Harmondsworth, Middlesex, England

First published in the United States of America by Greenwillow Books, 1989
Reprinted by arrangement with William Morrow and Company, Inc.
Published in Puffin Books, 1992
1   3   5   7   9   10   8   6   4   2

Text copyright © Susi L. Gregg Fowler, 1989
Illustrations copyright © Marisabina Russo Stark, 1989

LIBRARY OF CONGRESS CATALOGING-IN-PUBLICATION DATA
Fowler, Susi L.
    When summer ends / by Susan Gregg Fowler ; illustrated by
Marisabina Russo.   p.   cm.
    Summary: A young child is sorry to see summer end until she
remembers all the good things the other seasons bring.
    ISBN 0-14-054472-0 :
    [1. Seasons—Fiction.]   I. Russo, Marisabina, ill.   II. Title.
[PZ7.F8297Wh 1992]   [E]—dc20   91-40425

Printed in Hong Kong by South China Printing Company (1988) Limited
Set in ITC Mixage Medium

When summer ends I will cry and cry.

Why?

Because everything good happens in summer.

Like what?

Like the Fourth of July,
and watermelon,
and splashing in the
front yard pool,

and cousins coming—
and frogs and flowers—
and berries and
wearing shorts!

What about autumn?

I don't like autumn.

What about Halloween?

Oh.

What about piles of
crisp leaves to jump in?

Oh.

And the first frost, and fires in the fireplace, and Thanksgiving turkeys, and pumpkin pies?

Oh.
I guess I like autumn.

What about winter?

I don't like winter.

What about Christmas?

Oh.

What about building fat snowmen,
and tasting snowflakes, and being
so bundled up even Grandma doesn't
know who you are?

Oh.
I guess I like winter.

What about spring?

I don't like spring.

What about Easter?

Oh.

What about watching
the geese come back?

Oh.

And pussy willows, and flying your kite, and flowers poking through the snow,

and lots of puddles everywhere,
and new boots for wading?

Oh.
I guess I like spring.

When will summer be over?

Soon. Why?

Because nothing good
ever happens in summer.